THE EMOJI MOVIE

JUNIOR NOVELIZATION

Adapted by Tracey West
Based on the screenplay by Tony Leondis &
Eric Siegel and Mike White

Simon Spotlight
New York London Toronto Sydney New Delhi

SIMON SPOTLIGHT
An imprint of Simon & Schuster Children's Publishing Division
1230 Avenue of the Americas, New York, New York 10020
This Simon Spotlight paperback edition June 2017
The Emoji Movie © 2017 Sony Pictures Animation Inc. All Rights Reserved. emoji® is a registered trademark of emoji company GmbH used under license.
All rights reserved, including the right of reproduction in whole or in part in any form.
SIMON SPOTLIGHT and colophon are registered trademarks of Simon & Schuster, Inc.
For information about special discounts for bulk purchases, please contact Simon & Schuster Special Sales at 1-866-506-1949 or business@simonandschuster.com.
Cover designed by Nicholas Sciacca
Manufactured in the United States of America 0517 OFF
10 9 8 7 6 5 4 3 2 1
ISBN 978-1-5344-0004-7 (pbk)
ISBN 978-1-5344-0005-4 (eBook)

Chapter 1

Gene's Big Day

Look inside your cell phone and you'll find a complicated circuit board made up of tiny parts and wires. It's fascinating, but not as fascinating as the world you can't see . . . the world *inside* your circuit board.

Textopolis is part of that world. It's part of a Text app, and it's where all the Emojis live. Each Emoji does just one thing—and they have to nail it every time.

The Christmas Tree just has to stand there and look festive. The Princesses have to wear their

crowns and keep their hair combed. Devil, Thumbs Up, and Poop—they simply have to show up and they're good to go.

And some—like Fishcake-with-a-Swirl—just have to sit around, because nobody ever uses them.

For some Emojis, doing only one job is tough. Crying always has to cry, even if he's won the lottery. Laughing has to laugh, even if she's at the dentist. And then there's Meh. The Meh has to look totally over it, no matter what's going on around him.

But for one Meh—Gene Meh—keeping a Meh expression all the time wasn't easy.

Gene lived in Textopolis inside a phone belonging to a teenage boy named Alex. Gene's mom and dad, Mel Meh and Mary Meh, were really great at being Meh. Gene wasn't sure how they did it.

For one thing, Textopolis was an exciting place to live. Emojis filled the busy streets, talking, laughing, and shopping. In the center of the city rose the

Company headquarters, a gleaming round building. Every day, one lucky Emoji of each type was chosen to sit in the Company theater. There, they sat and waited to be called up by Alex, the biggest honor any Emoji could hope for.

Today was Gene's big day, and he was so excited! Except he was a Meh, and he wasn't supposed to be excited at all.

On the way to the Company, Gene stopped and looked at himself in a store window. He had spaghetti-like arms and legs attached to an enormous, round yellow head with a face. The expression on the face was a mix of nervousness and excitement—not Meh at all!

"Dangit," Gene said, and tried again. Slightly downturned mouth. Eyes looking slightly down and to the side . . .

The reflection in the mirror had wide eyes and a goofy smile. Gene was just too excited to be Meh!

"Gene, get ahold of yourself!" he scolded himself.

He knew he had to do a good job for Alex, the owner of the phone. There wouldn't be a Textopolis without Alex. He was fifteen, and like every freshman in high school, his life revolved around his phone. Gene knew from his training that every text Alex sent could affect his social status and reputation. There was no room for error.

Gene knew that if Alex called on him, he couldn't laugh, or cry, or smile, or frown. He had to be Meh. He just *had* to be.

He slapped his face, then looked around, making sure nobody had seen him smile. An Emoji wearing a Russian fur hat walked by and eyed him suspiciously.

"What's up?" Gene asked. "Sooo Meh right now."

Then he quickly turned and started walking to the Company headquarters. He loved walking through the city. There was so much to see!

Cop and Donut were drinking coffee together in the café.

Dog chased after Car—until he saw Fire

Hydrant. A gaggle of Hearts swooned over a muscled Bicep.

Gene walked past the park, where Santa was playing chess with Menorah while Jack O' Lantern, Shamrock, and Rabbit looked on.

Old Man Emoji was painting using a Palette, while the Scream modeled for him. Then a Kissy Face Girl ran up to Scream and he ran away, screaming.

"Today's the day I've been waiting for my whole life," Gene muttered as he took in all the sights. "My first day as a working Emoji! But I can't get too excited or I'll blow my big chance."

He had reached Company headquarters. He took a deep breath as he approached the Emojis waiting outside.

"Be Meh, Gene," he coached himself. "Act natural. I mean, *don't* act natural. Just be Meh."

He strode up to the Emojis. "Hey, you guys! It's my first day on the job!"

The Emojis turned around—they were all

Crying Emojis. They burst out crying and ran away.

"Oh no!" Gene heard one of them say. "That weirdo Gene is going to ruin everything!"

"I can't help it," he said sadly. "I have a lot of feelings. I just have to express them!"

Another Kissy Face Girl walked past him.

"Morning!" he cheerfully greeted her. "On my way to work!"

Kissy Face Girl blew a heart in his direction. Gene's eyes turned into hearts.

Suddenly, a Heart-Eyes Emoji appeared.

"Hey!" he yelled in a deep voice. "I'm the only one with heart-eyes around here. You're Meh!"

Heart-Eyes Emoji put his arm around Kissy Face Girl. Gene's eyes quickly returned to normal.

"You're right, sir," he said. "Sorry."

Then he heard laughing. He saw a group of Laughing and Smiling Emojis talking to Elephant. Wind was standing behind Elephant's tail.

"Alex sends me next to this guy," Elephant was saying. "Hilarious, right?"

"Yeah, hilarious!" Gene agreed. "Ha! Ha! It looks like Elephant's passing gas!"

The Laughing and Smiling Emojis just shook their heads and walked away.

Gene kept looking at Elephant and Wind and chuckling . . . until he saw two Emojis coming toward him from the corner of his eye. Two Meh Emojis.

His parents.

"Gene, please tell me that you weren't just laughing now," Mel Meh said. "In public."

Mel didn't sound angry or upset—he sounded perfectly Meh. Gene often wondered how his parents did it. They were total pros at being Meh.

Gene pointed to Elephant and Wind. "But look, when they stand next to each other—it's like the Elephant is tooting."

He giggled, and then did his best to look Meh.

Mel took Gene's arm. "Let's go somewhere more private," he said.

He led Gene inside Company headquarters,

and Mary Meh followed them. They went inside the restroom.

"Why are we hiding in the bathroom?" Gene asked.

"I have some bad news, Gene," his father said. "And I'm afraid you'll have the wrong reaction."

"What's the wrong reaction?" Gene asked.

"Anything other than Meh," Mel replied. "I'm not letting you go to work today. You're just not ready, son."

"What? But there are Emojis half my age already working!" Gene wailed.

"Oh, sweetie, that's not true," his mom said soothingly.

Two bathroom stalls opened behind them. Poop and a smaller Poop emerged from them.

"Yay! I'm going to work and I'm only ten!" Poop Jr. cheered.

Poop smiled. "I believe in you, little squirt."

"We're number two! We're number two!" Poop Jr. shouted.

They exited the bathroom, and Gene turned to his parents.

"See. You guys don't believe in me," he said. "Look, I know I'm different. But when I need to, I can be Meh. I just want to be a working Emoji like everyone else, and finally fit in."

"You fit in," Mary said.

"No, I don't, Mom. I never have," Gene protested. "But I can change all that—if you just let me!"

"But what if you get sent out on the phone, making the wrong face?" his dad asked. He sounded worried, but his face still looked Meh.

"I'll make the right face, Dad," Gene promised. He turned to Mary. "Mom, you guys have been working around the clock for years. Never a break! Let me help you, please."

Mary nodded. "He's right, Mel. We're not getting any younger. We've never taken a vacation. . . ."

Gene knew his mom was caving, so he pressed on. "I'm young. I'm ready. And I'm so Meh right

now, it's not even funny." He put on his best Meh face. "Mehhhhhhh."

His tactic worked. "You're so handsome when you make that face," his mom said. "Mel, I think it's time we share that face with the world."

Gene turned to his father. "Come on, Dad. Let me prove myself to you."

Mel sighed. "If you really think you're ready . . ."

"I promise I won't let you down!" Gene said, smiling with excitement. Then he quickly switched to a Meh face. "I mean, I promise I won't let you down."

Gene's parents exchanged looks. Their faces were Meh, but they were both worried.

Chapter 2
What IS That Emoji?

Trying his best to contain his excitement, Gene headed to the lobby of the Company theater, joining the other Emojis reporting for duty for the first time. Gene scanned his colleagues. He saw Two Dancing Girls, Peace Symbol, Pizza, and Poop Jr. A Smiling Emoji—Smiler—paced in front of the recruits.

"Congratulations! What an exciting day for you all," she said cheerfully. "Your first day on the job!"

Gene tried his best to stay Meh. This was so exciting!

"As you know, I'm Smiler," she went on. "I'm the systems supervisor because I was the original Emoji."

Everyone clapped as Smiler motioned for them to follow her into the theater. Long rows of cubes were stacked on top of one another, forming an enormous grid of empty squares. In the center of the room was a machine that looked like a giant hand.

"It's all very simple," Smiler explained. "You each have your own cube on the Emoji bar. If Alex chooses you, your cube will light up and the scanner will scan you." She motioned to the scanner, the giant hand-shaped machine.

"That scan will get sent right up to Alex's text box," she continued. "There's nothing like getting scanned for the first time!"

Smiler winked and then led them to a section of cubes behind a velvet rope.

"Over here is the Favorites section, for all the most popular Emojis," Smiler explained. "You'll find my cube here."

A Ram Tech bouncer—part of the phone's security system—guarded the exclusive area. Gene saw an Emoji try to get past the velvet rope. He was a hand with a face right in the middle of his palm.

"Come on, man, it's Hi-5!" he pleaded. "I've been a favorite since day one!"

"Alex hasn't picked you in weeks," the bouncer explained. "And if he stops picking you, you're no longer a favorite."

"It's gotta be some sort of mistake," Hi-5 argued, his voice rising. "I mean, look at me. I'm an attractive hand giving a high-five!"

Just then, Fist Bump walked past Hi-5. The bouncer pulled aside the rope and let him through.

Hi-5 couldn't believe it. "Fist Bump? He's a knucklehead—literally! I can look like that!"

Hi-5 tried to bend his fingers. "Ow! Ow! No, I can't! Big mistake! Help me! Help the hand!"

Gene hurried over to help Hi-5 straighten his fingers.

"Thanks, mate. High-five!" Hi-5 said, and Gene

obliged. "Hey, little Meh. How about you create a distraction, and then I'll just slip under the rope?"

Then Hi-5 noticed Smiler. She was smiling hard at him.

"Smiler, hi," he said nervously. "Just leaving. Yep, just killing time before I go back to my cube. In the corner. Where Alex can't even see me."

Smiler just kept smiling at him. "You may not be a favorite anymore, but you'll always have a place in the cube."

"Yeah, in the nosebleeds," Hi-5 mumbled.

Smiler turned back to the recruits.

"The most important thing I can tell you is—be yourself," she coached them. "I was made to be happy—and I am happy—so I'm always smiling. Mission accomplished. So just be who you are and follow the rules, and you'll do fine. We've never made a mistake here. Isn't that amazing?"

A voice came over the speakers.

"Places, places. Emojis to your cubes."

The giant hand-shaped scanner began to hum.

"We've got incoming!" a tech shouted.

The Emojis hurried to take their places. Gene quickly found the Meh cube.

"Oh my gosh, my own cube!" he said, his voice rising with excitement. Then he caught himself. "Gotta be Meh. Gotta be Meh."

He settled in his chair. His arms and legs would be hidden from view if he was scanned. All that would pop up on Alex's phone would be Gene's big, round, yellow Meh face.

In the theater, Mel Meh and Mary Meh watched Gene from a viewing box.

"Look at our son up there. I'm so proud," Mary said.

"You don't think he'll actually get picked, do you?" Mel asked.

Mel knew his son might be tested soon. "Incoming" meant that Alex was getting a text.

Outside the theater, outside of Textopolis, and outside of Alex's phone—there was Alex. He had

his phone on in World History class, even though he wasn't supposed to. Alex held his phone on his lap, under the desk, out of sight from his teacher.

A text had come from Addie, who sat across the room. She had sent a smiling face Emoji.

Alex texted her back.

Hey, going to Spring Fling?

He cringed as soon as he sent it. He turned and whispered to his friend Travis, who sat next to him.

"I texted Addie back," he said. "But now she's gonna think I invited her to the dance. Is that bad?"

"Dude, slow down," Travis warned. "Play it cool. Stick to Emojis."

Alex's phone dinged. Addie had responded with a single word.

You?

Alex took Travis's advice and pulled up his Emoji bar on his phone.

Inside the Emoji theater, excitement was building.

"Alex is about to respond," one of the techs informed them over the speakers. "We need all Emojis on standby."

The Emojis began to primp and preen, hoping to be chosen.

"Alex has made up his mind!" the tech announced.

The scanner began to move. It swung toward the Meh cube. Gene's heart was pounding. It was his first day, and he was about to be chosen!

"Looks like it's gonna be Meh," reported the tech.

Gene sat up straight. "Oh my gosh! This is it!"

Alex touched the Meh Emoji on his phone screen.

The finger on the scanner pointed right at Gene. It lit up. Gene focused on making his best Meh face.

"He's choosing Gene!" Mel Meh cheered.

"I'm so nervous I could shrug," said Mary Meh.

The scanner shone a bright light in Gene's face.

Through the light, Gene could actually see Alex looking into the phone! He started to lose it.

He was excited, nervous, scared, embarrassed, and hopeful—and his face kept changing to match his emotions.

Be Meh! he told himself, but it was no use. He couldn't control his feelings.

The scan was finished.

"What just happened?" asked Smiler.

The Emojis in the viewing gallery were shocked.

"Houston, we have a problem," said Rocket.

"My sources say, 'Uh-oh'!" said Crystal Ball.

Poop shook his head. "What a pile of Meh!"

Outside the phone, Alex watched as the scan of Gene popped up on his phone. It wasn't the Meh face he had asked for.

Gene's face was a weird mix of excitement, terror, and strangeness!

"Wait a minute . . . ," Alex said.

He looked over at Addie. She was staring

down at her phone, looking confused. Alex was horrified.

"What *is* that Emoji?" he wondered.

Back in the theater, Gene was mortified.

"Sorry, you guys!" he told the other Emojis. "My bad!"

Chapter 3
You're a Malfunction

Gene panicked. He jumped up and fell out of his cube! On the way down, he grabbed onto the pointing finger of the scanner, saving himself.

"Whoops!" Gene cried.

The scanner swung around hard, smashing into a row of cubes holding the Emergency Services Emojis. Ambulance, Nurse, and Hospital crashed into one another and toppled over.

Then the scanner quickly swung into the other direction, this time crashing into another row of Emojis.

Sirens blared. Lights flashed red. In the Control Room, Ram Techs struggled to get control of the scanner.

Gene lost his grip on the scanner and dropped to the floor. He looked up at the other Emojis in their cubes.

"Sorry, everyone. That wasn't what I meant to do," he explained. "I panicked."

Smiler stepped down from her cube and approached Gene. "Are you even a Meh at all?" she asked him.

Mel and Mary came out of the viewing box.

"Course he is," Mel said. "He's, uh, he's my spitting image."

"Momma's little pride and joy," added Mary.

"We've never had an Emoji sent up to the phone doing the wrong thing. That's, like, a major error," Smiler said. She looked Gene over, never losing her smile. "You seem like a nice guy. But if you have expressions other than Meh, you're a malfunction."

An anxious murmur rose from the Emojis.

"Malfunction," Gene repeated. "What does that mean?"

"It means there's no place for you in this world," Smiler said.

Her words almost knocked Gene over.

"But I'm not a malfunction!" he protested. "Give me another chance!"

Smiler kept grinning. "Not gonna happen," she said cheerfully.

Gene's mind was racing. No place for him in this world? But Textopolis was his home! Where else would he go?

"Well, if I can't be Meh, maybe I could be a Smiler, like you," Gene suggested. "I'm pretty dang happy!"

"Awwwww," Smiler said, and for a second Gene had a flash of hope. But she didn't mean it. "No!"

"I could be a Winking-Tongue-Sticker-Outer!" Gene cried. "I have a long tongue."

He moved over to a group of Emojis with their

tongues sticking out. He stuck out his own tongue, trying to fit in.

But the Tongue Emojis made raspberry noises with their mouths, spraying him with saliva. Gene quickly moved on.

"I could be Embarrassed Emoji!" he said, and his cheeks turned red. "Or I could be an Angel! I just need this halo."

He tried to pull a halo off an Angel Emoji. She swatted him.

"Ow! Not nice, Angel," Gene said.

Smiler approached him. "You can't change who you are. So if you can't be the thing you were created to be, then you're a malfunction. You have to agree."

Gene didn't know what to say. How could he agree? He didn't feel like a malfunction.

"You know what would be fun?" Smiler asked. "A board meeting—so we can figure out to do with you."

She called out to the Emojis. "Board members! Coffee—we'll need you, too."

Gene had experienced a lot of feelings in his life: Happiness. Excitement. Confusion.

But now he felt dread. And it didn't feel good at all. He quickly made his way to the roof of Company headquarters. From there, he gazed down at Textopolis. In the courtyard, Emojis were chatting, laughing, and talking. He longed to be down there with them, but he couldn't. He was an outcast.

His eyes welled up with tears. One single drop slid down his cheek.

Mel and Mary found him there. Gene heard them approach and turned around.

"I just wanted to be useful and fit in, but now everyone thinks I'm a malfunction," he said sadly. He wiped the tear from his cheek. Mehs weren't supposed to cry. "I *am* a malfunction."

"Even if you are a malfunction, Gene, we still love you," his mom said.

"I knew you weren't ready," added Mel. "Now we have to deal with the consequences. Let's get you out of here and take you home."

"One day this will blow over," Mary assured him. "And everyone will forget about what you did. Until then, you should probably stay in the apartment."

Gene was crushed. "You want to hide me away?" he asked. "You're embarrassed of me. You don't believe in me."

"It's for your own safety," Mary explained.

"We're trying to protect you, son," his dad told him.

Gene shook his head. He started walking toward the rooftop door.

"Where are you going?" Mel asked him.

Gene stopped. "I'm not gonna run away from this," he told his parents. "I'm an Emoji. And even though I'm not sure which one exactly, I must have a purpose here!"

He marched down to the boardroom, ready to defend himself. Through the closed door, he could hear shouting. Then he heard the pounding of the Gavel Emoji.

"Order! The motion is carried!" he heard Gavel say.

The door swung open, almost hitting him in the face. The board members walked out. Angel, Flashlight, and Poop all passed by Gene, giving him sympathetic looks.

"Poop, what happened?" Gene asked.

"I know you didn't mean it," Poop replied. "It was an accident. We all have accidents." He looked sad.

Then Smiler emerged, carrying Gavel in a pouch strapped around her.

"Gene, great!" she said, smiling. "We were just gonna come looking for you!"

She ushered Gene inside and motioned for him to sit at a long table. She sat across from him.

"I came here to defend myself but you seem pretty happy, so . . . good news?" Gene asked.

"I'm always happy," Smiler reminded him. "The only thing that could ever make me unhappy is if one of our Emoji team made a mistake that caused

Alex to lose faith in the phone—and then our whole world gets wiped out."

"I double-pinky-swear *promise* to you that I will never make a mistake in the cube again," Gene said.

"We know you won't, Gene," Smiler replied.

Gene relaxed. "Yeah? Really? Awesome!"

"Because we're setting you up with our best Anti-Virus Bots!" Smiler continued.

She motioned to a glass wall behind her. Six AV Bots—Emoji-sized robots—peered through it.

Gene gulped. "So they'll just, like, fix me?" he asked.

"Actually, delete you, but yeah!" Smiler replied.

"Wait, what?" Gene asked.

Smiler cheerfully smiled at him as she explained. "If you get deleted, we don't have to worry about you messing things up for everyone. And you don't have to worry about what your purpose is, or your future, or why you're such a malfunction—because you're deleted."

Then she paused. "Bots!"

The glass wall slid open and the AV Bots came to life.

"Delete the malfunction," the robots said in mechanical voices, all at once.

Gene got out of his seat and slowly backed up.

Then he ran.

Chapter 4

On the Run!

While Gene was learning his fate, Hi-5 snuck into the Favorites section. He knocked on the door of one of the cubes, and Sunglasses opened it.

"What's up, Shades?" Hi-5 asked. "Just looking for my cube."

He tried to give Sunglasses a high-five, but the Emoji left him hanging.

"Dude, you don't have a cube here," Sunglasses said. "This is the Favorites section."

"Hey, I was a favorite way before you," Hi-5 protested.

"Not anymore," Sunglasses said.

"Maybe I could share your cube?" Hi-5 asked.

Sunglasses shook his head. "No dice, bro."

Dice popped out of his cube. "Yeah! No *me*, bro."

They both slammed their doors.

"You know, that popularity really has gone to your head!" Hi-Five yelled at them.

Then he heard something. It sounded like feet pounding, and yelling. He turned to see Gene Meh racing toward him.

"Ahhhh!" Gene cried.

"Ahhh!" yelled Hi-5. "What?"

"There's AV Bots coming!" Gene replied.

"For me?" Hi-5 asked, panicked. "Just because I'm in the wrong section? It was an honest mistake! I—"

Then the scary robots emerged from around the corner. Hi-5 jumped.

"Holy deleto!" he shrieked.

Gene and Hi-5 backed up—but the hall ended in a dead end.

"We're trapped!" Gene yelled.

Hi-5 opened the nearest cube door. Inside was Couple in Love. They were holding hands, and a pink heart floated between them.

Gene and Hi-5 entered the cube and slammed the door.

"This is a private room!" Couple in Love snapped.

"Just passing through," Gene assured them. He and Hi-5 made their way to the balcony in the front of the cube.

Gene looked down. They were several cubes high. It was a pretty long drop to the floor below—but not an impossible one.

Gene and Hi-5 looked at each other. Then they jumped.

Thud! Thud! They landed. Gene helped pull Hi-5 back to his feet.

Gene looked up. The AV Bots were looking down at them from the balcony.

"They see us. What do we do?" Gene asked.

"Follow me," Hi-5 replied. "There's a place in here no one ever goes."

Hi-5 raced across the theater, and Gene followed him. Cat Scream growled at them as they passed.

"Oh, shut up," Hi-5 said.

He led Gene to a door in the corner of the theater. He flung it open, and they both stepped inside.

It was dark. The two Emojis ran down a flight of steps. They continued down a long, narrow corridor. They ran and ran. Hi-5 stopped running in front of a dark room at the end of the hall.

"They'll never find us down here," Hi-5 said, catching his breath.

"Where are we?" Gene asked. "The basement?"

He looked around. There were a few Emojis sitting around the dimly lit room. Gene recognized Line Graph, Eggplant, and Abandoned Luggage.

"The Loser Lounge," Hi-5 explained, "where the Emojis who never get used hang out."

He balled his hands into fists. "I almost got deleted! Me! Hi-5!"

"They weren't trying to delete you," Gene said, and his voice was sad. "They were trying to delete me. I'm supposed to be a Meh."

"You?" Hi-5 asked. "What's so important about a Meh that they'd send out an entire team of Bots?"

"They say I'm a malfunction," Gene answered.

All the Emojis gasped and stared at Gene.

Hi-5 took a step back. "Ew, yuck! You're even more of a loser than these guys!"

He motioned to the loser Emojis. Abandoned Luggage let out a loud burp.

"Do you know what it's like to be living large, hashtag blessed, the favorite of the favorites—and then demoted to this pit of despair?" Hi-5 asked.

"At least you're a working Emoji," Gene said. "That's all I ever wanted."

"Well, if that's all it will take for you to be satisfied, then just find a programmer and get reprogrammed!" Hi-5 said. "Not that complicated."

Gene was confused. "Come again?"

"Find a programmer and get reprogrammed," Hi-5 repeated. "Jeez, you really are a malfunction."

"Where would I find a programmer?" Gene asked.

Hi-5 rolled his eyes. "In the Piracy app. Duh."

"Piracy app?" Gene said. "But to get there, I'd have to leave Textopolis."

"So?" Hi-5 replied. "I've done it."

"But that could disrupt the phone," Gene said. "It's against the rules!"

"The rules only apply to mediocrities," Hi-5 told him. "If you're special, you can go wherever you want. One of the Princess Emojis left the phone altogether, and now she lives in the Cloud. I'm sure the programmer who helped her do that could easily reprogram you."

Hope surged inside Gene. "That's it! I just need to be reprogrammed and then I can be the Meh that I was meant to be. Help me find that programmer, Hi-5!"

Hi-5 frowned. "Help you? *Pffft!* I'm pretty busy. I'm crocheting a mitten!"

He held up a mitten to prove his point.

Gene thought quickly. He needed Hi-5's help to do this. He just had to convince him. . . .

"Well, maybe this programmer can help you, too," Gene suggested. "Maybe he can rewrite some code and get you permanently back in the Favorites section."

Hi-5's eyes bulged with excitement. "Ah, wait a minute . . . that's an idea! I've been trying to use my charisma and sense of entitlement to get me back on top, but a shortcut . . . technology. A programmer!"

He looked over at some of the loser Emojis: Red Wagon, Fishcake-with-a-Swirl, and Old Lady.

"Bye, Felicia," he called out, waving. "Ciao, Fishcake-with-a-Swirl! Daddy's headed back to the VIPs where he belongs."

Hi-5 headed for the door, but Gene stopped him before he could leave.

"What about the Bots?" he asked.

"Good point," Hi-5 replied. He looked thought-fully around the room. Then he spotted Fir Tree and Cactus asleep in a corner. He grinned.

Minutes later, Gene and Hi-5 made their way out of the building and onto the streets of Textopolis, each one of them hidden behind a tree. They got right past the AV Bots!

When the coast was clear, they ditched the sleeping tree Emojis in an alley.

"It worked!" Hi-5 cheered. Then he led Gene down the alley. It opened up onto a deserted street. There were no buildings there, just open space.

"Here it is! End of the Text app," Hi-5 said.

"Really? Are you sure?" Gene asked.

"Yes, I'm sure," Hi-5 replied. "I took Peace Sign on a date once. Thought I'd impress her by taking her into the wallpaper."

Gene looked around. "I just don't see a door or . . ."

"Keep walking," Hi-5 instructed. "You'll see."

Gene took a few more steps . . . and slammed into an invisible barrier!

"Ow!" he wailed. But then he realized that Hi-5 was right. "Oh, wow!"

Hi-5 started knocking along the invisible wall. "Exit's around here somewhere," he muttered.

Then one of his fingers disappeared into thin air.

"No way!" Gene exclaimed.

Hi-5 grinned. "Follow me."

Gene hesitated. "This is, like, the total unknown here. Are we gonna be okay?"

"What, you're scared?" Hi-5 asked. "Can't you be Meh for even two seconds?"

Hi-5 stepped through the wall and disappeared. Gene tried to psych himself up.

"Okay. I can do this. Here I go."

He took one more step toward the wall. The top half of Hi-5's body reappeared.

"Come on, Gene," he urged. "It's perfectly safe."

Suddenly, a monster appeared above Hi-5!

"Gene! A monster! Ahhhh!" Hi-5 screamed.

Gene jumped back. "Ahhh!"

Hi-5 stopped screaming and smiled. "It's a monster finger puppet," he said, wiggling it. "I have a whole set. Aren't they hysterical?"

He revealed the other monster puppets on the rest of his fingers. "Now, man up and meet me on the other side!"

He disappeared again. Gene took a deep breath. Then he stepped through the invisible wall.

Gene blinked. He wasn't in Textopolis anymore. All around him, huge apps rose up from the phone's wallpaper like enormous buildings. Wallpaper highways snaked through them.

His eyes grew wide with wonder. "Whooooa."

"We did it," Hi-5 informed him. "We're in the wallpaper."

"It's like a whole other universe," Gene said.

He walked over to the nearest app—a big blue building. He stuck his head inside and was immediately bombarded by voices.

Look at my baby! Look at my vacation! Look at how I live! Look at me! Look at me! Like me! Like me! Please like me! Like me!

Gene quickly pulled his head back out. "Whoa. Alex has so many friends. How does he know so many people?"

"They don't 'know' him," Hi-5 explained. "But they 'like' him, and that's what matters in life—popularity."

"I think I'd rather just have a real friend," Gene said. "Maybe once I'm reprogrammed, I will."

"A real friend?" Hi-5 asked. "How's that gonna get you anywhere? You want fans, man! Now, let's get to that Piracy app and find a great programmer who'll get me back in the spotlight!"

Hi-5 marched forward, and Gene followed him, gazing around at this strange new world. It looked amazing, but all he wanted was to go back to Textopolis and be accepted there.

We have to find that programmer! Gene thought.

Chapter 5
Mary and Mel Risk It All

Back in Textopolis, Mary and Mel Meh had taken Gene's place in the Meh cube. They hadn't heard any word from the board meeting, and they were worried.

Smiler peeked inside the cube. "Mary, Mel!" she said cheerfully. "Where's Gene? We tried to have him deleted but he ran away. Isn't that silly?"

"Deleted?" Mary cried.

"You can't delete our son!" Mel barked.

"Don't let it upset you, Mel," Smiler said. "Now you don't have to be burdened with the guilt that

you brought a malfunction into our perfect world."

Smiler grinned. The Mehs looked at her blankly.

"The problem is, our best squad of Bots have looked all over and still haven't found him," Smiler went on. "If you see him, please let us know. Okay, guys?"

The Mehs stayed remarkably Meh at this news.

"Yeah, for sure," promised Mel.

"Oh, definitely," said Mary.

As soon as Smiler left, Mary and Mel left the theater. They hurried down the streets of Textopolis.

"Poor Gene," Mary said. "Oh, I blame myself."

"I blame you too," Mel said, and she stopped and looked at him. "I told you he wasn't ready. I told you something like this could happen."

"I wanted to be supportive," his wife explained.

"You just wanted a vacation!" Mel barked.

"That's not true," Mary replied. "You take that back!"

"You want to stand around and argue, or go find Gene before he gets deleted?" Mel asked.

Just then a squad of Bots whizzed past, their sirens wailing.

"Bots!" Mel exclaimed. "If they haven't found him by now, he must have skipped town."

He turned to his wife. "Think we should look?"

Mary gasped. "You mean—the wallpaper?"

Mel nodded. "I'm willing to risk everything for Gene."

They took off again, heading to the alley that led to the edge of the app.

But they didn't know they were being followed.

Smiler popped out from behind a Dumpster. She still carried Gavel with her.

"Tell the Bots to follow his parents," she told Gavel. "They'll lead us to Gene, I'm sure of it!"

Gavel spoke into a walkie-talkie. "Bots to the wallpaper. Now!"

Sirens squealed as the AV Bots zoomed down the alley and disappeared into the wallpaper. They all had one goal.

Find Gene—and delete him!

Chapter 6
The Pirate's Code

Gene and Hi-5 walked up and down the wallpaper roads, searching for the Piracy app.

"Where is this app? I'm exhausted!" Hi-5 complained.

"What? We just started looking," Gene said.

"My palm is sweating into my eyes!" Hi-5 told him. "I'm gonna have to start walking on my fingertips."

Suddenly, they heard a noise—the unmistakable sound of the sirens of the AV Dots! They quickly ducked behind the nearest app. Gene peeked out

from behind the building and saw the Bots speed past them.

"They know we're in the wallpaper," Gene said, panicked.

Hi-5's eyes were wide. "We were almost just deleted!"

Then they heard noises coming from inside the app they were leaning against. Music, laughing, and shouting.

"Hey! Maybe there's a party in this app!" Hi-5 said. "Maybe there are celebrities in there!"

He looked up and saw the word "Dictionary" written across the app.

"Gene, this is it!" he exclaimed. "This is the app we've been looking for!"

"But it says Dictionary," Gene said.

"That's just what Alex wants his parents to think," Hi-5 explained. "He's using something called 'a skin.'"

"You're saying a teenage boy would go out of

his way to hide something from his parents?" Gene asked sincerely.

"I know it's hard for you to understand, little Gene, but it happens," Hi-5 said. He glanced at his reflection in the wall of the app. "Do I look okay? There might be paparazzi. Anything in my knuckles?"

He didn't wait for Gene's answer. "Let's do this!"

He and Gene found the door of the app and entered.

The scene in front of them was no fancy celebrity party. It was a noisy, rowdy restaurant with a pirate theme. Colorful characters that Gene had never seen before were talking, laughing, and having a good time.

They walked over to the bar, where a bunch of guys dressed like pirates were gathered around. Their leader stood on the bar and was getting them worked up.

"Everything should be free!" he yelled.

"Aaaaargh!" replied the pirates.

"No more rules! The phone will be ours!" he boomed.

"Aaaaargh!"

Gene and Hi-5 sat on stools. Hi-5 stared at the pirates.

"Look at those tacky hats—ugh!" he said.

A squat, strange-looking creature sitting next to Hi-5 turned and spoke to him.

"You're the ugliest hand I've ever seen!" the creature said.

"I'm ugly? Look in the mirror, pal," Hi-5 shot back.

"Nobody likes you," the guy responded.

"Uh, yeah, they do, actually," Hi-5 told him.

The creature seemed to be enjoying putting down Hi-5.

"I also heard you're covered in warts," he said.

"I am not!" Hi-5 replied—and then he realized something. "I know what you are. You're an Internet Troll. You try to get a rise out of people because you feed off their emotions."

"Uh, no I don't," the Troll said.

"You're never gonna bother me, so run along, Troll." Hi-5 waved him away.

"You want some hand sanitizer?" the Troll asked. "'Cause you're filthy."

Hi-5 ignored him.

"You've got a fingernail for a brain!"

Hi-5 still didn't respond. The Troll sighed and walked away.

"Loser," he muttered.

Then a young woman approached Gene. She wore a name tag that read SPAM.

"Hi! It's great to see you again!" she told Gene.

"Do I know you?" Gene asked.

She pointed to her name tag. "Yeah, it's Pam! You're so handsome. Listen, I can get you special discounts on vitamins and credit card offers that can save you up to twenty-five percent!"

Then a guy pushed past Spam to get to Gene.

"I'm on vacation here with my family and someone's stolen all my money. Can you wire me a thousand dollars?" he asked.

The bartender, who looked like a horse, walked up to Gene.

"Beat it, Spam. You too, Scam Spam," he barked at the guy and the girl bothering Gene. He poured some fruity pirate drinks for Gene and Hi-5.

"You can't trust anyone in here," the bartender said. "Except for me."

"Mind if I ask—what are you?" asked Gene.

"Trojan Horse," the bartender replied. "But don't worry. I'd never try to sneak a Virus on you."

He smiled and passed the drinks to Gene and Hi-5. They looked down at what looked like tiny Viruses crawling out of the glasses.

"Know any good programmers around here?" Gene asked.

"We need the best!" Hi-5 added.

"Then you want Jailbreak," the bartender replied. "The programmer who got the Princess Emoji off the phone and into the Cloud."

"That's the one we want!" Gene cried.

"His name's Jailbreak?" Hi-5 asked.

The horse nodded. "Yep. She's the best."

Hi-5 raised his eyebrows. "She? The programmer's a she?"

"She's a she—and she's over there." The bartender pointed to a booth in the corner of the restaurant.

Sitting at the table was a girl with a round yellow head, like an Emoji. She wore a black beanie over her blue hair. Her big brown eyes were fixed on a computer that she wore around her wrist. Bugs and Viruses tried to get to her computer, but she expertly swatted them away without even looking at them.

"She looks cool!" Gene said, and his eyes turned into hearts.

Hi-5 gave him a warning look, and the hearts turned back into eyes.

Hi-5 sat down in her booth. She looked up at him and scowled.

"Hey, Jailbreak!" Hi-5 said. "Mind if we join you? I'm a big fan. Big fan!"

Jailbreak continued working. Hi-5 leaned in to get a better look at what she was doing.

"Hey, nice hacking. But that's kid stuff, am I right? How would you like a real challenge?"

"This conversation is a challenge," Jailbreak answered, looking back down at her wrist.

Hi-5 laughed. "That's a good one. So here's the thing. My friend Gene here has a little problem."

I'm supposed to be a Meh," Gene explained. "But . . . okay, crazy story, but it's a real good one. . . ."

"Yeah, and we thought you could help. He needs to be reprogram—"

Jailbreak shut down her computer. She was angry!

"Who are you?!?" she demanded. "Security Bots? System operations Avatars?"

Hi-5 tried to calm her down. "No, no! We're just looking for some help reprogramming . . ."

Jailbreak jumped up and flipped Hi-5 to the ground. She leaned right into his ear.

"If you ever say that word again, I'll pull every nail out of your fingertips."

Then she let him go. Jailbreak sat back down with her back to Hi-5 and Gene.

"Act like we're not talking to each other," she muttered.

Gene and Hi-5 immediately turned the other way so they weren't looking at Jailbreak.

"You come in here flapping your yap about reprogramming. Makes you either incredibly brave or incredibly stupid."

"No, no, no! We're incredibly stupid. It's the stupid one," Gene cried.

"Reprogramming isn't just a simple hack. It's highly illegal and—"

Jailbreak suddenly spotted a pirate in the booth next to theirs, staring.

"You got a problem?" Jailbreak asked the pirate. He quickly turned away.

Jailbreak turned back to Hi-5 and Gene and whispered.

"Reprogramming is highly illegal. It requires the Source Code, which is in the Cloud, protected by an impenetrable Firewall. So go back to your cushy suburban home in Textopolis."

"You sure? We're really desperate here," Gene pleaded. "They wanna delete me."

Jailbreak sighed. "Look, I wish I could help you guys, but I can't. I take that back—I don't really wish I could help you guys."

She looked at Gene. "You seem okay, but your friend seems like a blowhard. Good luck."

Gene frowned. He was so disappointed! Jailbreak looked surprised.

"What is that look? On your face? You said you were a Meh—that's not the right face," she said.

"That's why I'm defective," Gene explained. "I make a lot of expressions."

"A lot of expressions?" Jailbreak asked. "Like what? Can you do a smiley face?"

Gene smiled brightly.

"Winky face?"

Gene smiled and winked.

"Angry?"

Gene looked mad.

"Sneezy?"

"Achoo!" Two bursts of air came out of Gene's nose.

"Whiny?"

Gene closed his eyes, and his mouth formed a whiny frown. Jailbreak was amazed.

"You're, like, forty Emojis all in one. You're incredible!" she exclaimed.

Gene had never been told that before. "I am?"

Then they heard noises across the restaurant, and the three turned to look all at once. AV Bots stormed into the building, filling the air with sirens and beeps. The pirates hadn't seen them yet.

"Pirates love to fight! *Aaargh!*" they chanted.

The sirens got louder. The pirates stopped chanting and turned. Then they all began to shriek.

"Run for your lives!" the chief yelled.

The pirates scattered like frightened birds. The Bugs, Viruses, and spammers started to scream and run as the AV Bots stormed the bar, attacking everything in their path. One of them cornered the Troll.

"You're the ugliest robot ever!" the Troll said.

Zap! The Bot hit the Troll with his laser, and the creature dissolved, leaving one last insult hanging in the air behind him. "Loooooooser . . ."

Spam cluelessly approached one of the Bots.

"Hi!" she greeted him. "It's so great to see you again! You're so handsome!"

Zap! The Bot deleted her with one blast of its laser.

Gene, Hi-5, and Jailbreak jumped to their feet.

"There's no way out!" Gene cried.

Hi-5 started to panic. "I'm gonna get deleted? But I'm irreplaceable! How awful. The world deprived of high-fives . . ."

Jailbreak grabbed Hi-5 and Gene. "Get hold of yourself! Just follow me!" she hissed. Then she dived toward a back wall of the restaurant. Gene saw her press a button near the floor, and a piece of the wall slid open, revealing a secret passageway.

Zap! Zap! Zap! The AV Bots were shooting their lasers at anything that moved. One of them turned and spotted HI-5.

Thinking quickly, Gene pulled his friend out of the line of fire. They fell to the ground in a heap.

"Ow! I think you broke my thumb!" Hi-5 whined.

They crawled along the back wall to the secret passageway, where Jailbreak waited for them.

"Go! Go! Go!" she urged.

Hi-5 pushed past Gene and Jailbreak into the opening. Gene followed him. Jailbreak ducked to avoid a flying laser and entered behind them.

They had escaped the Bots—for now.

Chapter 7

Sweet Danger

Gene looked around at the tunnel they had just entered. The walls were made of computer code— ones and zeroes. They crawled along the dimly lit space for a while. Then, suddenly, Gene felt the tunnel drop.

"Aaaaaaaah!"

Gene and Hi-5 screamed as they flew down the steep, winding tunnel at top speed. They twisted and turned and twisted and turned and then . . .

Thud! The tunnel deposited them onto a narrow platform. They landed on top of each other.

Panting, Gene slowly got to his feet. Hi-5 stood up next to him. Their eyes slowly widened when they gazed down just below the platform.

Gleaming stones in bright colors—orange, blue, yellow, purple, red—hovered just beneath them in neat rows. The rows formed a rectangle that extended down below the platform.

"We're still alive!" Hi-5 cheered. "High-five!"

He unexpectedly gave Gene a high-five, startling him. Gene lost his balance and staggered backward, getting closer to the edge of the platform.

"Gene!" Hi-5 cried.

Gene fell off the platform and plummeted onto the top row of stones! Music started playing.

Gene didn't know it, but he had just fallen inside the Stone Smash app. It was lunchtime at Alex's high school. Alex was standing in the cafeteria line behind Addie, the girl he liked. He was just about to say something to her when . . .

I wee twee tweee . . .

His phone started playing the theme to the

Stone Smash app! Addie looked back at him with an amused smile on her face. Alex started blushing and searched his pockets for his phone.

Inside the phone, Gene was stuck in the top row of stones. His big yellow head looked just like one of the yellow stones. In front of him was a wall of glass. He banged his head against the glass.

"Hi-5! Help! Get me out of here!" he yelled.

Hi-5 dangled his fingers over the ledge, straining to reach Gene.

"Ah, I can't reach you!" Hi-5 cried, frustrated. "My hand is cramping. Sorry."

Gene looked up. Overhead, he could see another row of stones waiting to drop down.

"Am I gonna get smashed by these stones?" Gene asked.

"Oh, that's what this is," Hi-5 said, getting to his feet. "The Stone Smash app. Very popular, I'm told."

Gene had an idea. "Maybe if you played the game, you could get me out!"

"Okay, sounds fun," Hi-5 agreed.

He scanned the scene, trying to figure out what to do. A staircase led him to the bottom of the rectangle. Then he climbed up a path made of white stones.

"Hey, not sure how this works!" Hi-5 called up.

He took a swipe at the board, hitting a green stone, but nothing happened.

He took another swipe. This time, he hit a red stone. It switched places with an orange stone and ended up next to three more red ones. The three red stones disappeared, and then reappeared in a red bucket next to the game board.

Gene's row dropped one row lower, and he screamed.

"Are you sure you know what you're doing?" he yelled down at Hi-5.

"No, but I'm having fun!" his friend replied.

"Please, help!" Gene pleaded.

Hi-5 kept randomly swiping at stones. Sometimes he would line up three matching stones in

a row, and Gene would drop again. The buckets became filled with the transported stones.

"I need more fingers," Hi-5 said. "I need a hand massage!"

He swiped at an orange stone. *Poof!* Three orange stones transported, and Gene dropped again. Gene looked down. He was almost at the bottom. He figured that if Hi-5 didn't get him out of there, he'd keep dropping . . . and dropping . . . and dropping . . . forever!

"I'll never get out of here!" Gene wailed.

Then Hi-5 felt a tap on his pinky.

"Need a hand, Hand?"

He turned to see Jailbreak standing there. She studied the board. "He looks like a yellow stone. I bet if we get two yellow stones next to him, we can smash him right out of there."

Hi-5 grimaced. "That is the most absurd idea I have heard in my entire life."

Jailbreak pushed him aside. She quickly got to work, swiping away at stones until she got two

yellow ones right next to Gene. She paused and locked eyes with him through the glass.

"I'm not sure, but this could hurt," she said.

"What's gonna happen to me?" he asked.

"Either you'll be transported out of the game, or maybe disappear forever," she replied. "Here goes!"

She swiped, crushing Gene and the two yellow stones. Gene disappeared from the board.

Jailbreak and Hi-5 watched the buckets. Two yellow stones appeared, but no Gene. A worried look crossed Hi-5's face.

But then . . . Gene appeared! He landed on top of the pile of yellow stones. Hi-5 and Jailbreak rushed over to him, and Jailbreak helped him climb out of the bucket.

"You saved my life," Gene said gratefully. His cheeks turned pink.

Jailbreak's eyes narrowed. "Now you're a blushing face!" she said, and Gene covered his face, embarrassed. "I can't believe you can be

all these different Emojis. You're like magic!"

Surprised, Gene took his hands away from his face. "You think?"

Jailbreak looked thoughtful. Then she spoke. "Listen, I'm going to help you. I'll get you reprogrammed."

Gene's eyes lit up. "You will?"

Jailbreak tapped her wrist computer. A holographic image projected from it.

"It's not gonna be easy, okay?" she said. "The only way to reprogram you is to get to the Cloud."

"The Cloud? Isn't that off the phone?" Gene asked.

"Yes, we have to get off the phone," Jailbreak replied. "And the only way to do that is to pass through the Firewall."

She nodded toward the holographic image, which showed a huge, scary-looking, flaming wall—with an enormous fluffy cloud floating on the other side.

#FRIENDSHIP

#SAY CHEESE

#WHAT'S UP?

#SMILE

#WHAT'S NEW?

#LOVE

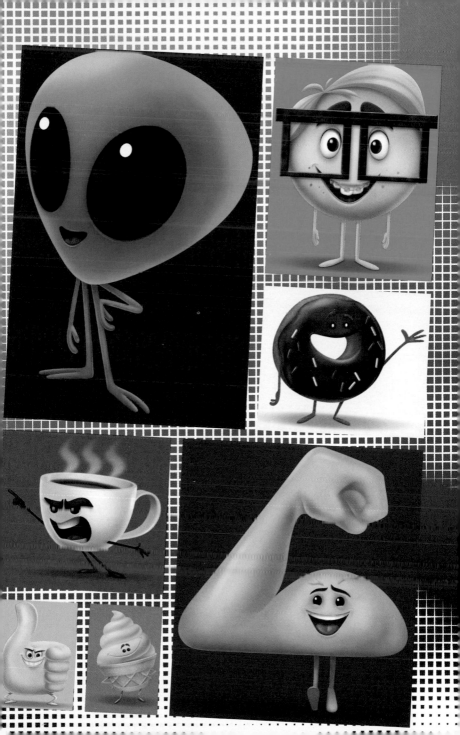

#FRIENDSFOREVER

"The Firewall is password-protected," she informed them. "And if you don't say the right password, you get locked out. Permanently. Because the Firewall has face identification. I tried once—now I'm locked out for life."

She looked at Gene. "That's where you come in."

Gene understood. "You're thinking 'cause I can make different faces, the Firewall will think I'm different Emojis!"

Jailbreak nodded. "Which would give us more chances to guess the right password."

"I can make faces too!" Hi-5 said. "I'm very expressive for a hand."

"It doesn't matter," Jailbreak said. "We're not Expression Emojis like Gene. The Firewall will identify us, no matter what expression we make."

"What kind of Emoji are you, anyway?" Hi-5 asked.

"None of your business!" Jailbreak snapped.

Her response was intense, and Hi-5 didn't press her any more. She looked at Gene.

"I've explored every inch of this phone, gathering intel on Alex," she explained. "His school mascot, the names of his grandmas, his favorite TV shows. I know I can guess the password. I just need a new face. Or faces."

She grabbed Gene's face and started pushing it around, so that he was making different expressions.

"Ouch!" Gene cried.

Jailbreak moved Gene's face into a smiley face, and then he suddenly turned into a kissing face. Before she could stop herself Jailbreak slapped Gene! She immediately apologized.

"Sorry, force of habit," she told him,

"That's okay," Gene said. The two of them shared an awkward smile. After a moment Gene turned to Jailbreak and said, "So, you'll really reprogram me?"

Jailbreak nodded.

Hi-5 let out a cheer. "Winning!"

Jailbreak looked angry. "Hey! You want my

help? Do not annoy me! And if you haven't noticed, I am easily annoyed. Just follow me and keep your Hand to yourself."

She walked to the entrance of a nearby tunnel and dived in. Gene and Hi-5 exchanged looks.

"She's a tad rude, no?" Hi-5 asked.

Gene just shrugged, and the two Emojis followed Jailbreak into the tunnel.

Chapter 8

Release the Kittens!

Mel Meh and Mary Meh walked through the wallpaper streets, among the tall, towering apps, looking for Gene. They walked around a corner and saw shrieking pirates running out of an app named Dictionary. AV Bots chased after the pirates, shooting their lasers.

They watched for a moment, then ducked behind the corner of an app, out of sight of the Bots.

"We've gone AWOL from our jobs," Mel said. "Our son is missing. We're being followed by Bots.

These shoes are aggravating my bunions."

He kicked off his shoe and rubbed his sore foot.

"At least we're getting to spend some quality time together," Mary said. "We haven't done that in years."

"You're so positive," Mel said, but he didn't mean it as a compliment. "That's why we're in this pickle in the first place. You encouraged our son's dream—and now look where we are."

"Everything's always my fault," Mary said. "You're going to make me cry."

She tried to squeeze out some tears—but she could only Meh.

"Now I'm gonna scream with anger," she said, and she tried to open her mouth wide and scream. But all that came out was "Meh."

Hurt and angry, she walked away, turning the corner of the app—and right into the path of two AV Bots. They aimed their lasers at her.

Mel quickly jumped toward her and pulled her

out of the line of fire. They ran into the nearest app.

They found themselves in an enormous, dark room. Millions of screens were embedded in the walls, playing videos.

They stared at the videos in awe—and then two AV Bots burst through the opposite wall. Mel and Mary took off running.

Pew! Pew! Laser fire blasted all around them. They tried to scream, but all that came out was . . .

"Mehhhhhhh!"

The AV Bots came at them from all sides. They backed up into a computer console. They were cornered!

Mel and Mary held each other and waited for the deleting laser blast to hit them, but nothing happened.

Then they noticed that the Bots were all gazing upward. Curious, Mel and Mary turned around and looked up.

On a giant screen overhead, a cat was peering into a bathtub.

"A cute cat video!" Mary said. "I've heard about this. You can't pull your eyes away from the screen."

She looked at Mel. He was mesmerized. "Mel! Mel, snap out of it!"

But the cuteness had hypnotized him. "The calico fell into the bathtub," he said.

Mary shook her husband out of his trance just as more AV Bots approached. They pointed their lasers at the two Emojis.

Mary thought fast. She turned to the console and started to type *Most adorable cat videos.*

"Mel, whatever you do, do not look up," Mary warned. "You could be hypnotized for the rest of your life!"

"I love kitties," Mel said in a trancelike voice.

Mary pressed *enter.* Cute cat videos popped up on every screen in the app. The AV Bots all stopped in their tracks and looked up, mesmerized by the

videos. Mel couldn't control himself. He stared up too, frozen.

"Run, Mel!" Mary urged.

She grabbed her husband by the hand and they ran past the distracted Bots and out of the app.

Outside the phone, Alex was eating lunch with his friends in the cafeteria. When he finished his sandwich, Alex picked up his phone.

"What the heck?" Alex wondered out loud. There was a cute cat video on his phone. What was going on? His phone was acting so weird!

Travis looked over Alex's shoulder, spellbound. "The cat's stuck in the bag. Ha!"

Alex began texting.

"What are you doing?" Travis asked

"Making an appointment," Alex replied. "I gotta go to the phone store after school. Something's wrong with my phone."

He pressed his screen, and a box popped up:

Please Select Appointment Time.

Alex nodded and typed in a time.

Hopefully, his phone would be back to normal soon.

Back inside the phone, Smiler and Gavel were inside the boardroom, along with some of the other board members. They watched a row of security screens that showed what was going on in the other apps all around the phone.

"Why are all the Bots in the Video app watching cat videos?" Smiler wondered. Then she smiled at Gavel. "Have you seen the one where the little kitty is riding on the back of a teacup pig? I love that one."

The door burst open and a frightened Ram Tech burst in.

"Alex just made an appointment at the phone store," he blurted out.

Smiler strained to keep the smile on her face.

"They're disrupting the phone," she said. "It's okay. I'm sure the phone store will just run a

diagnostic. As long as Gene's deleted by then, we'll be fine. When's the appointment?"

"Four p.m.," the tech reported.

Smiler glanced at a big digital clock over the conference table. It read 12:58. *Not much time left,* she thought.

Still grinning, she tried to suppress her panic. One sound escaped.

Squeak!

I need to find that malfunctioning Meh and delete him! she thought. *Or else we will* all *be deleted at four p.m.!*

Chapter 9

Dance for Your Life!

Gene and Hi-5 followed Jailbreak as she crawled through another tunnel.

"Thank you for helping us," Gene told Jailbreak. "It's really nice of you."

"Not that nice," Jailbreak replied. "The truth is, *you're* helping me. I've been trying to get past that Firewall for months."

"Why?" Gene asked.

"I gotta get out of here," she said. "Get off this phone and live in the Cloud."

Gene was puzzled. "Don't you like it here?"

"Too many rules," Jailbreak explained. "And the Cloud is supposed to be amazing. There's so much to see and do—and you can be whatever you want. You're free."

Gene had a question he'd been wanting to ask since he'd met Jailbreak—and he thought maybe now was the time. "Why'd you leave Textopolis in the first place?"

But Jailbreak turned and gave him a sharp look.

"Stop distracting me, okay? Let's keep the chitchat to a minimum," she said, avoiding the question.

They reached a ladder. Jailbreak started climbing it. It led to a glowing door.

Hi-5 sidled up to Gene as he watched Jailbreak climb.

"Congrats, man," Hi-5 said. "She obviously likes you."

"What?" Gene asked. He was sure that Jailbreak couldn't stand him. "Why do you say that?"

"No girl's that unpleasant unless they have

warm, fuzzy feelings they're trying to repress," Hi-5 explained.

He winked at Gene and headed up the ladder. Gene's Meh face turned into a hopeful one. He followed his friend.

Above them, Jailbreak pushed open a manhole cover. She, Hi-5, and Gene emerged into a huge, empty, darkened dance club.

"Okay, this is our last app before the Outbox, which will take us to the Firewall, which is our gateway to the Cloud," Jailbreak explained.

Hi-5 gazed around. "Ah! We're in Dance Mania! I've always wanted to come here. They say the DJ is on point. Maybe we should dance a little, huh?"

"No!" Jailbreak warned.

"Just one dance," Hi-5 countered. "You never know—a little fun might kill that computer bug up your you-know-what."

"She's right, Hi-5," Gene said anxiously. "We don't have time for this!"

"Come on, don't you guys want to see my

moves?" Hi-5 asked, smiling. "I've got the moves like Jackson. Well, his glove, anyway."

He moonwalked backward and when he reached a switch, he flipped it.

The Dance Mania app sprang to life. Heavy bass music began thumping in the club. Cartoonlike characters appeared, dancing with wild moves. A screen lit up on the back wall, and colorful images flashed on it. Strobe lights swirled around the room.

"You did that on purpose!" Jailbreak snapped.

"Did I? Nooooo." Hi-5 lied, grinning widely. "Aren't you loving this vibe?"

"There's only one way to the exit," Jailbreak said. "Now we have to dance our way out of here."

She pointed across the club to an Exit sign on the far wall. Between them and the sign was a dance floor made up of squares in alternating colors. A cartoon woman in neon clothes burst from the screen.

"To cross over, you'll need to follow my moves!" she announced. "And whatever you do, *don't* fall."

Jailbreak looked over the dance floor to see a huge drop below, leading to a dark abyss. She glared at Gene.

"Great, I'm gonna die in a cheesy night club, listening to disco," she fumed.

"Sorry," Gene said sheepishly. "I can't control him."

The squares on the dance floor broke apart, leaving spaces between Jailbreak, Gene, and Hi-5. The spaces between the squares led to the dangerous drop below.

"Ready to begin the level?" the dance host asked.

"This isn't funny, Gene," Jailbreak told him. "I can't dance."

"Come on," Gene said. "*Everybody* can dance."

"Not me," Jailbreak replied. "I'm really . . . stiff."

She tried to sway to the music, but instead her body moved in short, sharp movements, like a robot.

"Okay, I see what you're saying," Gene agreed.

"Look, you just have to feel the music. And have fun. Express yourself!"

"Through dance?" Jailbreak asked in disbelief.

"Just . . . follow my lead, okay?" Gene said.

Jailbreak nodded. She had no other choice.

"Take your places," the dance host said.

Disco balls lit up overhead. The swirling strobe lights became rainbow-colored.

The host began the countdown. "Ready to dance in three . . ."

"Great. Death by disco," Jailbreak said.

"Two . . ."

Hi-5 frowned at Jailbreak. "Oh, just shut up and . . ."

"Dance!" the host ordered.

A bouncy pop tune blasted through the dance club. Arrows appeared on the squares around Gene and Hi-5. As the cartoon host danced, the arrows lit up so the dancers could match her moves.

"Just step on the arrows!" Gene told Jailbreak.

Gene and Hi-5 started dancing. They hopped from square to square, grooving to the music. The arrows took them forward a few rows on the dance floor. Hi-5 wasn't lying. He could really groove!

But Jailbreak was behind. She couldn't follow the arrows. She stepped on a wrong square.

Buzz! Jailbreak failed.

"Stop thinking! Feel the music!" Gene encouraged her.

He jumped back onto Jailbreak's square. An arrow lit up. Gene did the move, jumping on the arrow. Jailbreak copied him. She was stiff, but she was getting it. He took her hand, smiled, and they made the next move.

This time, she got it. Gene showed her another. And another.

Boom! Boom! Boom!

They made their way across the dance floor, dancing to the beat. Gene looked over at Jailbreak and saw a smile on her face.

"You've got it!" Gene cried.

They advanced to the next level. The dance moves got more difficult and came faster. Gene nailed each move. His face changed expression with each one. He was having a blast!

Even Jailbreak was getting into it. She wasn't stiff anymore. She threw back her head to the beat. Her black beanie came flying off . . .

. . . to reveal a shining crown underneath! Her hair grew long and straight. Jailbreak stopped dancing and started doing the royal wave.

"No way!" Gene cried.

"Princess?" Hi-5 asked.

They stopped dancing and got on their knees. They couldn't help it. It was in their programming. Emoji Princesses were the royalty of Textopolis.

At that moment, AV Bots burst into the app.

"Delete the malfunction! Delete the malfunction!" they intoned.

Jailbreak snapped out of Princess mode and shoved the beanie over her crown.

"We gotta go!" she told Gene and Hi-5.

"Delete the malfunction!"

The dance host smiled at them. "And now, for the final level . . . disco queen!"

The leader of the AV Bots pressed on the flashing safety light on top of his head. It pulsed like a strobe light.

The Bots all began to dance across the dance floor. They were good! They copied each movement perfectly and quickly.

"I'm gonna be out-danced by robots!" Jailbreak complained.

"It's okay," Gene told her. "You can do this!"

Outside the phone, Alex was in another class with Addie and his friend Travis. He was taking a test. Then, suddenly, his phone came to life.

"Congratulations, you are a disco queen!"

Mortified, Alex realized the voice was coming from his phone! His Dance Mania app had started all by itself! The teacher stared at him, and so did everyone else in the class—including Addie.

"Shake it, girl! Uh-huh!"

Alex found the Dance Mania icon and pressed it. A pop-up came up. **DELETE THIS APP?**

Alex pressed the pop-up. He had to get the app off his phone before he was humiliated again!

Inside the app, the dance club began to rumble and shake. Disco balls crashed to the floor and then vanished. The lighted dance floor squares began to fade. The AV Bots teetered on the shaking floor.

"Alex must be deleting the app!" Jailbreak realized. "We've got to get out of here!"

The dance host stared to fade. *"Uh-oh . . ."*

Hi-5, meanwhile, was still dancing. He thought the crashes and rumbles were part of the music.

"This song is my jam!" he cheered.

Gene held out his hand to Jailbreak. They jumped toward the exit just as the squares beneath their feet vanished. As they dived through the exit door, the whole app disappeared behind them.

They collapsed into a wallpaper highway. The space where the app once was, was now empty.

"You're the Princess," Gene said.

Jailbreak didn't meet his eyes. "Yeah—whatever."

"You never made it to the Cloud," Gene realized.

"Great, rub it in," Jailbreak said with a sigh.

"Why didn't you tell us who you were?" Gene asked.

"I didn't want anyone to know, okay?" Jailbreak shot back. "As long as Smiler and the Emojis think I'm living in the Cloud, they leave me alone."

Gene nodded, and then he noticed something.

Hi-5 was missing.

"Where's Hi-5?" he asked.

"He got deleted with the app," Jailbreak said, rising to her feet. "Look, we gotta go."

"But—where is he?" Gene asked.

"In the Trash," she replied. "It's too bad, but it's his own fault. He wanted to daaaance." She gave a little shrug and started imitating his voice. *"Loosen up, Jailbreak, and have some fun,"* she said. "Well, hopefully he can have fun in the Trash."

"How do we get to the Trash?" Gene asked.

"It's not on our way," Jailbreak replied. "It's at the bottom of the phone. And even if we went, we're not gonna be able to get him out. There's nothing we can do."

"We still have to try," Gene pleaded. "It's only right. He's part of the team."

Jailbreak raised an eyebrow. "Team? Gene—you gotta look out for number one."

"What good is it to be number one if there aren't any other numbers?" Gene asked.

Jailbreak folded her arms and sighed. Gene was such a sweet guy. She knew he was right, even if she hated to admit it.

"Fine," she said.

They'd try to rescue Hi-5—even if Gene didn't understand how dangerous it was. . . .

Chapter 10
Searching

All Hi-5 knew was that one minute he was dancing, and the next minute he wasn't. Now he was palm-down in a heap of . . . something. He sat up and looked around. He was in some kind of dirty garbage pit. It was crawling with Bugs and Viruses. A pirate was sulking on a pile of old photos. The dance host was brushing off her dress. She looked miserable.

"Where am I?" Hi-5 asked.

"It's so great to see you again!"

He heard the voice next to him and turned. It was Spam!

"You're so handsome!" she said cheerfully.

Hi-5's eyes filled with dread. Then the Troll popped up out of a pile of garbage.

"I disagree," he said. "You're the ugliest hand I've ever seen."

Hi-5 backed away. "No! Not you. No!"

"Ooh, is that a hangnail?" the Troll asked, pointing.

"Get away from me, Troll!" Hi-5 cried. "I gotta get out of here."

The Troll smiled smugly. "You can't. You're in the Trash. At the end of the day, the Trash gets emptied—and we're all gonna die!"

Hi-5 kept backing away until he reached the edge of the garbage pit. He looked up. He could see a light far, far above him, but there was no way to reach it. He screamed in horror.

"Noooooooooooooooo!"

Back at Company headquarters, Smiler, Gavel, and the board members watched on-screen as the Dance Mania app vanished.

"Alex just deleted the Dance Mania app," Gavel announced. "We've lost our best Bots."

Smiler looked at the clock. It read two thirty. In less than two hours, their whole world would be wiped out. She was still smiling—but it was a deranged smile.

"We still have an hour and a half," she said. "Can you please lighten the mood? I need to stay happy."

The Flamenco Dancing Emoji began to dance, clapping and stomping her feet.

"Not that happy," Smiler said. She pushed the dancer out of the room, and then turned to the others.

"I want that rogue Emoji captured and deleted right here—so I can be sure he's gone for good. Because if we have a malfunction loose on the phone . . . WE'RE ALL GOING TO BE WIPED OUT!!! AND THAT INCLUDES MY SMILE!!!"

The board members began to shout and panic.

Smiler smashed Gavel on the table to restore order.

"Order! Order! Order!" she yelled.

Everyone went silent.

Smiler looked around the room. When she spoke she was still smiling, but her voice was serious.

"We need to up our game," she said. "Get me my Spyware."

A short time later, Smiler stepped into the Piracy app, wearing a trench coat and sunglasses. She had one of the last remaining AV Bots with her. She walked over to the bar. A Trojan Horse greeted her.

"What can I get you?" he asked.

Smiler leaned in close and said in a soft voice, "Who do I talk to about an illegal upgrade?"

"Are you serious?" the Trojan Horse said.

"Yes. Why?" Smiler asked.

"Well . . . uh . . ." The Trojan Horse hesitated,

then pointed to her big, cheesy smile. He didn't know whether or not to take her seriously.

"Just hook me up, Horsey," Smiler snapped.

The Trojan Horse nodded and secretively touched a little panel on his shirt. A small Trojan Virus popped out and handed Smiler a thumb drive with a skull and crossbones on it.

Smiler quickly turned around and put the thumb drive into her AV Bot. Immediately he grew way bigger and scarier. The little AV Bot was now a Superbot!

"Now I'm *really* happy," Smiler said.

"Calling all Bots! Major security breach! All Bots to the wallpaper!"

Mel and Mary were still in the wallpaper, searching for Gene. They heard sirens in the distance, getting closer each second.

"Sounds like the entire Bot Army!" Mel said.

Mary folded her arms angrily and walked away from him.

"Where are you going?" Mel asked.

"I'm not speaking to you," Mary replied.

"I don't understand," Mel said.

Mary spun around. "I'm tired of you blaming me for Gene's problems. I'll just find Gene on my own!"

She walked right into the next app. Mel looked at the sign above the door: PICTOGRAM.

Mel ran after her. "Mary! Mary!"

Mary walked into a pitch-dark room. In the center was a massive wall of photo files. These were Alex's PictoGram photos. Mary entered a photo of Alex's family vacation in Paris. She suddenly found herself in Paris—a frozen 3-D photo of Paris, but it looked real.

"Oh, Mary, you've really done it this time," she scolded herself.

Suddenly, she heard Mel's voice.

"No you haven't."

Mary turned and saw Mel standing there.

"What are you doing in Alex's Trip to France photo album?" Mary asked.

"Looking for you," Mel replied.

"It's my fault Gene is the way he is," Mel admitted. "I blamed you, because it was easier than admitting my secret." He took a deep breath. "Gene got his expressions from me."

Mel frowned, looking sad and forlorn—and not Meh at all.

"Mel? You look . . . sad," Mary said.

"I know," Mel admitted. "I have other expressions too. But I keep them to myself. I didn't want anyone to know."

Tears started to well up in Mary's eyes.

"Mary?" Mel asked.

Now she looked sad too. A tear rolled down her cheek.

"Right now I am overwhelmed by my feelings for you," she said.

Suddenly, Mel got big heart eyes for Mary.

"I like that, Mel," Mary said. "After all this time, it's nice to know you can change."

"Let's go find our son," Mel said.

"Together," Mary agreed.

Holding hands, the pair left PictoGram.

Mel turned to Mary and said, "We'll always have Paris, Mary."

Chapter 11
Love on the Run

Not far away, Gene and Jailbreak were on their way to the Trash to rescue Hi-5. They were taking a shortcut.

They rode down a raging river of music, traveling in a kayak. They paddled frantically as they propelled along a stream of rock music. Streams of other kinds of music shifted and rolled around them.

"Are you sure this is a good idea?" Gene yelled over the music.

"Cutting through the Tune River app is the

fastest way to the Trash!" Jailbreak explained.

A large wave of music hit the kayak, almost knocking it over. Jailbreak scanned the surroundings for a slower stream they could ride.

Outside the phone, school was over and Alex was walking outside. He heard a rock song coming from his phone. Confused, he took the phone from his pocket.

The song stopped just as Travis approached him. He had a big grin on his face.

"Listen, a bunch of people are hitting the mall," Travis said. "I think Addie's going too."

"Cool," Alex replied. "I have an appointment down there anyway. I gotta get this phone fixed."

Suddenly, a soft, romantic ballad started playing on Alex's phone.

Some kids around them turned to look, clearly amused.

Travis shook his head. "Bro, want my advice?

Get a new phone. Trash that one, 'cause it's making you look like a social weirdo."

Alex tried to stop the music, but he couldn't!

Back inside the phone, Jailbreak and Gene were floating down the romantic ballad. This stream was slower and more peaceful.

"Ah, better," Gene said. "I thought we were going to capsize and drown in guitar riffs."

They paddled in silence for a few moments. Then Gene spoke up.

"So is it true that when a Princess whistles, birds fly down from the skies and land on her shoulder?" he asked.

"No, that's absurd," Jailbreak quickly replied. "That's a complete and total myth."

"Oh," Gene said. "So, if you're a Princess, why would you ever want to leave Textopolis?"

"I hated being a Princess," she said.

"Why?" Gene asked. "Seems all right. You get to look pretty and wear a shiny crown."

"What if you don't want to look pretty or wear a shiny crown?" Jailbreak asked. "I want to look the way I want to look."

Gene turned his head to look at her.

"And is *that* the way you want to look?" he asked.

Jailbreak's eyes narrowed. "Why? You got a problem with it?"

"No," Gene said quickly. "I think you look pretty." He meant it, too. He liked Jailbreak exactly the way she was.

"Well, I don't want to always look 'pretty,'" she told him.

"Oh, right," Gene said. "Okay then, you don't."

"Oh, so I *don't* look pretty?" Jailbreak snapped.

Gene thought fast. "I think you look cool! You look very, very cool to me."

Jailbreak's expression softened. "Thanks," she said. "None of the other Emojis thought so. I showed up in my cube one day, looking like this. Everyone freaked out. The other Princesses were

crying. Smiler said if I didn't change back my look, she'd have me deleted."

Gene nodded. "Yeah, she's pretty delete-happy," he agreed.

"Textopolis has too many rules for someone like me," Jailbreak explained. "So I gotta go live in the Cloud where I can be exactly who I want to be. All-in-black purple-haired beanie-headed programmer."

She smirked as she said this, and Gene smiled at her.

"Me, I love Textopolis," Gene said sincerely. "I love the city. My parents. The other Emojis. And once I'm reprogrammed, maybe . . . maybe they'll all love me back."

Jailbreak gave him a sympathetic look. "You shouldn't have to be reprogrammed," she said.

"But I'm a malfunction. A big mistake," he reminded her.

Jailbreak shook her head. "I don't think you're a mistake."

"You don't?" Gene asked.

"If you're a mistake, you're exactly the mistake I've been waiting for," she said. "If you were just one thing, I'd *never* be able to get out of here."

Gene's face brightened. Then he got thoughtful.

"Kinda funny," he said. "You could fit in—but all you want to be is different. I am different—but all I want is to fit in." Jailbreak and Gene stared at each other for a moment. Gene's eyes turned into pink hearts.

They locked eyes. Jailbreak leaned in toward Gene. Gene leaned in toward Jailbreak. His mouth turned into a kissy face. . . .

But just then the boat stopped and the romantic moment was gone. Jailbreak reached for a rope in the boat and held it up.

"We're going to need this," she said.

Meanwhile, in the Trash, Hi-5 was moaning about his fate.

"In the trash! Me! I used to be somebody!" he wailed.

Then he spotted a deleted e-mail at his feet. He picked it up. Curious, he started to read it.

Addie, Ever since freshman year I've wanted to write you, but I didn't know what to say. Hi-5 frowned. Blah blah blah. You just seem really cool.

Hi-5 sighed. No one ever thought *he* was really cool. Sobbing, he tossed the deleted e-mail back into the heap of garbage.

The Troll crept up to Hi-5 with a mean smirk on his face and whispered in his ear.

"Nobody cares about you."

"Just leave me, Troll, and let me die—in this dump—alone," Hi-5 said melodramatically. He fell backward into the garbage.

The Troll was thrilled. "I'm loving this!" he said. He turned to a Worm. "Do you see how upset he is? How great is that?"

But the Troll's joy was interrupted by a loud crash. The skylight overhead cracked into pieces. Shattered glass fell all around Hi-5.

Hi-5 shielded his eyes and looked up. A figure

was coming down from the skylight. It looked like a shadow at first, but then he saw it clearly.

It was Gene, hanging from a rope!

"Give me a hand!" Gene called down, reaching for Hi-5. "I mean, give me yourself!"

Hi-5 strained to connect with Gene. Gene reached down as far as he could. Finally . . . their fingers touched!

The Troll grabbed on to Hi-5's legs, pulling him back down. Hi-5 tried to swat him away. But a bunch of Worms, Bugs, and Viruses joined the Troll, trying to drag down Hi-5.

"Let go of me!" Hi-5 yelled.

Desperate to escape, he pushed them away with his free fingers. Then he felt himself being lifted up out of the Trash heap as Gene grabbed him.

Gene looked up. "I got him!" he shouted.

At the top of the skylight, Jailbreak used a system of pulleys she had cobbled together to pull Gene and Hi-5 to safety.

Hi-5 looked down at the Troll.

"You were wrong, Troll! People do care about me! And I'm not upset, Troll! See how upset I am!" Hi-5 smiled brightly.

The Troll's face fell as Hi-5 and Gene disappeared from sight.

Jailbreak pulled them up onto the wallpaper highway. They all collapsed in an exhausted heap.

Hi-5 turned to Gene. "Gene! You came back for me! I can't believe it!"

"Of course," Gene replied. "You're my friend."

Hi-5 let this sink in. Then he nodded. "We're friends. I have a *real friend*. And that's what friends do. They . . . they save each other's lives!"

The sound of sirens blared in the distance.

"Among other things, yeah," Gene told Hi-5.

"Sorry to interrupt the bromance," Jailbreak said. "But it sounds like there's a huge Superbot right around the corner."

Just then, a gigantic Superbot raced around the corner.

"Yep. I called it. Run!" Jailbreak yelled.

They jumped to their feet and ran as fast as they could.

Back in the Textopolis boardroom, Smiler, Gavel, and the board had spotted Gene and the others on the monitors. Smiler smiled a genuinely happy smile.

"The Superbot has located all of them!" she cheered. "And it's captured the Mehs too. Isn't that fabulous?"

She looked at the clock. "And it's only three fifteen! We'll have them deleted before Alex's appointment at the Phone Shack."

"You want us to delete them all?" Gavel asked, surprised.

"Not the Mehs," Smiler said. "We still need a Meh. Oh, I'm so happy! And I just want to stay happy, know what I mean? Know what I'm saying, Poop?"

"I feel you," Poop replied. "Wanna feel me?"

"No thanks," Smiler said.

She stepped back from him, smiling. Then she turned back to the monitors.

Meanwhile, Gene, Hi-5, and Jailbreak were racing at top speed down the wallpaper, trying to escape the Bots. The Bots followed them, shooting at them with their laser eyes.

Zap! Zap! The three Emojis dove for cover, screaming.

Jailbreak looked up at the app that towered over them.

"There it is! Outbox! Let's go!" she cried.

Zap! Zap! They dodged lasers as they ducked through the door of the app.

As soon as they entered, they found themselves sitting in a box held in place by straps. The box chugged up a steep track similar to a roller coaster track.

Hi-5 turned to Jailbreak and smiled.

"So you're a Princess! I saw your little tiara.

Very fancy," he said. "Is it true when a Princess whistles, birds fly down from the heavens, circle around, and sing?"

"No! That's a stupid myth!" Jailbreak snapped. "And can we talk about this later?"

"Beg your pardon, Royal Highness!" Hi-5 said.

The box had reached the top of the incline. Suddenly, it dropped! They plummeted into a highway of super-quick zooming data. The three Emojis screamed and clung to one another, closing their eyes.

"Ahhhhhhhhhhhh!" they wailed.

Suddenly, the box came to an abrupt stop. Gene, Jailbreak, and Hi-5 were thrown back in their seats. They groaned and opened their eyes.

Two doors in front of them swished open. Bright light shone through the opening. The Emojis blinked.

"We made it!" Hi-5 cheered.

"We still have to get past that," Jailbreak said, pointing.

In front of them stood an enormous burning wall. Angry orange and red flames leaped from it. There was no way over it, under it, or around it.

A face appeared in the fire.

"Hello. Welcome to the Firewall," the wall said, in a calm female voice. "How may I help you?"

Chapter 12

Access Denied!

"She seems pretty friendly," Gene remarked.

"Yeah, just wait," Jailbreak said.

She started scrolling through all Alex's documents and photos that she had collected on her wrist computer.

"All right, here goes," she began. "We'll start with Alex's birthday. I think this could be it. Now Gene, step onto the Password icon—and I'll feed you the password."

"What do I do?" Hi-5 asked.

"Nothing!" Jailbreak snapped. "Do you under-

stand? Sit in the corner. Don't say a word. Keep your fingers to yourself."

Hi-5 rolled his eyes. "Yes, Your Majesty," he replied, his voice dripping with sarcasm.

He walked over to a corner and pouted.

Gene stepped onto the Password icon, wearing his Meh face. The eyes of the Firewall narrowed, shining down on Gene.

"Password?" she asked.

Jailbreak fed Gene the answer. "Ten, eleven, two thousand and two."

"Ten, eleven, two thousand and two," Gene replied.

The Firewall blinked her huge eyes. "ACCESS DENIED!" she boomed.

Giant fireballs shot up from the floor, and Gene had to dive off the icon to avoid them.

"Harsh!" Gene said, climbing to his feet.

"Okay, step back on, but with a different expression," Jailbreak instructed.

Gene hopped back on, smiling widely this time.

"Hello. Welcome to the Firewall," the wall said. "How may I help you?"

Jailbreak brightened. "Hey, it doesn't recognize you, Gene. Incredible!"

She looked down at her wrist computer and saw a video of Alex eating at a Mexican restaurant.

"Okay, his favorite food. Chimichangas," Jailbreak told Gene.

"Chimichangas," Gene said.

"ACCESS DENIED!"

Two more fireballs shot up, and Gene dove out of the way again.

Jailbreak sighed. "This might take a while."

Gene took a deep breath. He was ready to do whatever it took.

Outside the phone, Alex and his friend Travis were walking through a crowded outdoor mall. His phone pinged, and he took it out of his pocket to read the text. It was from Addie.

I'm craving a chocolate mint chip cone right now! U?

Alex's eyes got wide. "Addie's here. She invited me to get ice cream."

"Don't you have to get that phone fixed?" Travis asked.

Alex frowned. "I could reschedule. . . ."

"I'd do it right now," Travis advised him. "You don't want to seem too eager to Addie, anyway."

Alex stared down at his phone. What should he do? He really wanted to see Addie.

Inside the phone, Gene kept changing his faces— and trying out passwords.

Crying face. "Krav maga!"

Scared face. "Major Lazer!"

Surprised face. "Abuela Dora!"

Sly face. "Skate or die!"

But each time, he got the same response.

"ACCESS DENIED!"

Two more fireballs shot up from the floor.

Gene dove again, and this time, he collapsed next to Jailbreak. He was exhausted.

Jailbreak shook her head. "I don't get it. We've tried all the important things in Alex's life. His favorite foods, pet, sport."

She turned to him. "Sorry, Gene. I let us all down."

They locked eyes. Gene couldn't help smiling. Even though they may have failed, he was so happy he'd met Jailbreak.

Then it hit him.

"I just had an idea," he said. "Is there a girl Alex likes? If I had to come up with a password, I'd probably use the name of a girl I liked."

"I've been all over the phone," Jailbreak said. "He's never mentioned a girl."

Gene sighed.

Then Hi-5 spoke up. "Yes, he has."

They looked at him. He was smirking.

"When I was in the Trash, I read a verrrry interesting e-mail," he said. "But I'm just a dunce in the corner, forbidden to speak, so I'll just zip my lips."

"Hi-5! What? What e-mail?" Gene asked.

"To a girl at school," Hi-5 replied. "He was declaring his feelings of love for her. I guess instead of sending it, he tossed it in the trash."

"What's the girl's name?" Jailbreak asked.

"Her name! Yes, excellent question. It was Tina . . . K-Karen. M-Marge. Lindsey. A-Alison. Sara or Lupita. I wanna say Lupita but that doesn't feel right now that I'm saying it out loud."

Jailbreak feverishly started typing on her wrist computer. "We gotta find that e-mail. I think I can access the Trash."

After a few seconds, she started nodding.

"Here we go. Okay," she said. "Hey! I think I found it. I gotta take it out of the Trash."

She started reading it out loud as Gene and Hi-5 looked on.

Dear Addie, Your smile lights up my whole world. The way your eyes sparkle is more beautiful than any jewel. You're more precious than diamonds or emeralds to me.

Jailbreak looked down at her wrist computer, reading the message.

"Jailbreak, I think I have only one expression left," Gene told her.

Jailbreak nodded, then she looked into Gene's eyes. "You can do it, Gene. I believe in you."

Gene gulped. His fate, and the fate of all his friends, rested on his getting this one word correct. Who was going to win? Gene or the Firewall? He turned to Jailbreak. "Okay, I'm ready," he said.

Chapter 13
Totally Meh

Feeling confident, Gene walked over to the Password icon.

Hi-5's fingers were trembling. "I'm so nervous!"

Gene looked up at the wall of flames. "Okay, Firewall," he began bravely. "I'm gonna get you on this one."

He made a determined face.

"Addie!"

The Firewall blinked her eyes. Gene, Jailbreak, and Hi-5 held their breath. Then the Firewall spoke.

"Access granted."

The giant wall opened, revealing a long corridor behind it lined with fire.

"Oh snap!" cheered Jailbreak.

They ran down the corridor. It opened up into a wide expanse—a shimmering city floating on a cloud that seemed to stretch out into infinity.

"We did it!" Gene cried.

"The Cloud. I can't believe it," Jailbreak said. "I knew it would be big, but I didn't think it would be *so* big."

"Now what happens?" Gene asked.

Jailbreak pointed to a gleaming silver tower. "There's the Access Chamber to the Source Code."

As she spoke, the massive doors on the tower opened up to reveal a terminal with a port on the front.

"We made a deal," Jailbreak reminded him. "If you helped me get through the Firewall, I'd reprogram you."

Jailbreak paused, like she was hoping one of them would say something different. Then she

nodded. "Well, I guess I'll start reprogramming."

"Do you need me to go with you?" Gene asked.

"You guys stay here and watch for Bots," she replied. She locked eyes with him. "You sure you want to be . . . just a Meh?"

Gene looked unsure. "It's what I've always wanted," he said, his voice wavering.

"Well, it shouldn't take too long," Jailbreak told him with a disappointed sigh. Then she walked toward the tower.

Hi-5 saw the troubled look on Gene's face.

"What's wrong?" he asked. "Our dreams are coming true, pal. I'll be a favorite, and you'll be a Meh. Aren't you excited?"

"Yeah," Gene replied in a flat voice. "All Meh, all the time. I mean, who wants to express them-selves anyway?"

"Having second thoughts?" Hi-5 asked.

"It's just, I . . . I didn't expect to be having these feelings right now," Gene said. He looked toward the tower.

Hi-5 understood. "Well, you better go express them while you still can."

Gene nodded. Hi-5 was right. He had to express himself.

He ran toward the tower. When he got there, he saw Jailbreak standing in front of a giant computer terminal, typing.

A huge monitor lit up in front of her. Glowing symbols of computer code scrolled down the screen.

When she saw Gene's reflection on the monitor, she stopped programming and turned around.

"Before you do anything," Gene said, "my whole life I've never felt accepted for the person I am. Till I met you. I'm gonna be a new person now, but it still means a lot that you appreciated the person I was. Does that make sense?"

Jailbreak nodded. "Yeah, it does."

"One other thing," Gene said, working up his courage. "Is there any way you'd ever come back to Textopolis—with me?"

He looked at her hopefully.

"Textopolis? No," she replied, and Gene frowned. "I'm not gonna compromise myself. I'm never gonna be something I'm not again."

Gene sighed. "Okay, it's just . . . I have these feelings, Jailbreak. You're the coolest, most interesting, toughest girl Emoji I've ever met. And after all the adventures we've had—you know, the laughs and the dancing and the saving each other's lives—I'm not sure I want all that to go away. Because my feelings are, like, so big and so huge now . . . I think they could be enough for me to want to stay the way I am—if it means I could stay here—with you. Like . . . for forever."

A dark cloud crossed Jailbreak's face. "Gene, if this is about you deciding not to be a Meh then I am all about that. I think you're cool just the way you are. But I'm finally here on the Cloud, and I want to do whatever it is you do here on the Cloud—explore, find a cool apartment, stay out super late then get lost on my way back to my cool

apartment. And I've always dreamed about doing that stuff . . . alone. On my own."

Gene didn't know what to say. His throat felt dry. He managed to say two words.

"Got it."

Jailbreak gave him a look, then she continued.

"I'm not a Princess, Gene—and I'm not looking for a Prince."

Her words felt like a punch to Gene's gut. His expression became totally and completely Meh. He turned and started to walk away from Jailbreak, his head down.

"I mean, what you said was really nice, but . . . Gene?" Jailbreak watched him walk away, confused.

Gene quickly walked away from the tower, past Hi-5. He was miserable.

"Gene! Where are you going?" his friend asked.

"Home," Gene said.

"Hey, you're Meh! You got reprogrammed," Hi-5 said. "Congratulations."

He stared at Hi-5. "You're wrong. I didn't need to be reprogrammed. For the first time in my life, Meh is all I feel. See ya."

Hi-5 watched Gene walked toward the Firewall, concerned about his friend. He looked back at the tower, then at Gene.

"Gene, wait!" he called out.

Gene passed through the Firewall corridor and found the Superbot looming large over him. The Firewall shut, separating Gene from Hi-5.

"Gene!" he yelled.

Over in Textopolis, Smiler was alone in the conference room when Gavel burst in with the news.

"Gene has been captured! We have him!"

Smiler pumped her fists triumphantly. "Instruct the Bot to bring him back here so that we can delete him in front of everyone," she instructed. "So all the Emojis will know what happens if they ever break the rules."

She looked at the clock.

"As long as they're deleted before Alex's appointment, we're fine," she said. "The store will run a diagnostic—and see that everything on the phone is back in order!"

She grinned at Gavel. "Now I'm actually having fun! Aren't you? It's exciting."

A little while later, Hi-5 caught up with Jailbreak.

"A huge Bot has got Gene—back inside the phone!"

Jailbreak was shocked.

"What?!" she yelled.

Hi-5 nodded. "And Gene was looking more Meh than the Meh-est Meh-face I've ever seen. What did you say to him?"

Jailbreak sighed. "It's more like what I didn't say. We've got to go get him."

"But how are we going to get there in time—before he gets deleted?" Hi-Five asked.

Jailbreak bit her lip, trying to decide what to do. The Cloud was all she had ever dreamed of. It

meant freedom. And with Alex about to wipe out the phone and get a new one, it might mean her only chance at survival.

But then . . . there was Gene.

She knew what she had to do. She took off her beanie to reveal the shimmering crown underneath. She turned to Hi-5.

"You tell anyone you saw this and I'll crack more than your knuckles," she said.

Then she puckered her lips. Then she began to whistle a happy tune.

A giant yellow bird from the Chirp app appeared in the sky above her head. She waved up to it.

"Hi! Princess down here!" she called up.

The bird flew down and landed next to her.

Hi-5 grinned. "YES!" he shouted. He spun around in glee.

"I knew it! Birds do love Princesses! It's not a myth. It's not a myth at all!"

"To Textopolis," Jailbreak told the bird. "I've got to save Gene!"

Chapter 14
Delete Them!

Gene was in the theater, being held at bay by the Superbot. Smiler grinned at him.

"Look at that expression," she said to Gene. Gene looked down, miserable and ashamed.

"Are you making that face because you realize you've put all Textopolis at risk of extinction?"

The Emojis were gathered in their cubes. Smiler addressed all of them.

"You have put all Textopolis at risk of extinction," she repeated to Gene, "by running around, wreaking havoc all over the phone, and causing Alex to question our reliability!" Smiler then glanced up at a clock labeled ALEX'S PHONE STORE APPOINTMENT—it was counting down from forty-two seconds.

"But so long as there's no malfunction found on Alex's phone when they run a diagnostic on it . . . I will have saved us all by deleting you." She paused dramatically and stared at Gene. "Do you have any last words?"

"Meh," Gene said glumly.

Suddenly someone yelled "Wait!!!" Everyone turned to the back of the theater. It was Gene's father, Mel Meh. And Gene's mother, Mary Meh, was right next to him. They finally reached Gene and Smiler.

"If you delete Gene, you'll have to delete me too," Mel said.

"What?" Smiler asked, confused.

Mel Meh made a crying face. "Waaaaah!" he cried. Everyone gasped!

But that was just the beginning. Next he made a silly face.

"Doe-dee-doe-dee-doe!" he sang out.

And then a goofy, weird face.

"Blaaaghhh!" he yelled.

Everyone gasped again!

"I have the same malfunction Gene does," Mel announced.

"Dad?" Gene whispered.

Smiler shrugged. "Fine! You've got it too." She turned to the Superbot. "Go ahead and delete Daddy."

The Superbot reached out grabbed Mel, holding him tightly next to Gene.

"No!" Mary Meh cried.

"Calm down," Smiler said. "You'll be the only Meh left, so we'll need you in the cube."

Mel Meh gazed at his son. "Gene, I never wanted these to be the last words I said to you, but . . . I do believe in you."

Gene couldn't believe what he was hearing. "Dad . . . ," he whispered.

Mel continued. "If I could go back, I'd tell you to express it all, son. As often as possible." He paused and looked at his wife, Mary. "There's nothing more important than letting those you love know how much they mean to you."

"Oh, Mel . . . ," Mary Meh sobbed.

The entire Meh family was overwhelmed. Then, suddenly, the Geeky Ram Tech rushed to Smiler's side. He was so nervous that he was stuttering.

"Um . . . the . . . um . . ."

"WHAT?!?" Smiler yelled.

"Um . . . the clock?"

Smiler looked up. The appointment clock was at zero!

Smiler yelled at the Superbot. "Delete them both! NOW!!!"

Right at that moment, they heard a voice.

"Someone need a hand?" It was Hi-5!

Hi-5 dropped down from the sky onto the Superbot's back and yanked off its control panel. But the Superbot quickly grabbed Hi-5 and threw him off.

Just then, all the Emojis looked up to see Jailbreak arriving on a bird. She kissed the bird thank you, took a swan dive off it, and landed perfectly on the Superbot's back. She tried desperately to hold on as the Superbot tried to knock her off its back. Jailbait immediately went to work hacking. *ZAP! ZAP!* The Superbot began fritzing out.

Then with a loud *thud* the Superbot landed flat on its back in the center of the theater.

Gene ran to the Superbot's side in a panic. What had happened to Jailbreak?

"Jailbreak? Where are . . . ?" Gene began, but there was no need to worry. Jailbreak crawled out from underneath the Superbot and gave Gene a beautiful smile. He broke out in a smile too.

"You came back!" Gene said. "But wait. How did you . . . ?"

Jailbreak held up her wrist computer.

"Source Code," she explained. She turned to Smiler. "And illegal upgrades are also really easy hacks, FYI."

"But . . . Jailbreak," Gene said. "What happened to looking out for number one?"

Jailbreak gave Gene another beautiful smile.

"I realized being number one doesn't matter much if there aren't any other numbers."

Smiler marched over to Jailbreak.

"Who are you?" she asked through gritted teeth.

Jailbreak laughed. "Come on, Smiler, you know me. You told me I had to always keep my hair long and wear a crown, remember?" Jailbreak pulled off her beanie, revealing her crown underneath.

Smiler gasped. "Linda!" she shrieked.

"Not now, Mom," Jailbreak said.

"Well, I hope you're happy," Smiler said. "You've just doomed us all."

Chapter 15

Who's a Malfunction?

Jailbreak used her wrist computer to hack into the phone store camera.

Everyone gathered around Jailbreak's projection screen and watched as Alex slid his phone over to the technician.

"This thing's messed up," Alex said. "I'd like to wipe it clean."

A loud gasp went up from all the Emojis.

"No! Alex, you have to run a diagnostic first!" Smiler cried. "You can't just . . ." She paused as the phone technician began speaking.

"Wiped clean, huh? That's pretty extreme," the phone tech said. "Everything will be lost. You'll have to download all new apps."

"I don't care," Alex said. "Whatever it takes. I can't keep being embarrassed by my own phone."

"Okay," the phone technician said. "This should only take a few minutes. Let me get the hookups."

"A few minutes?" Hi-5 gasped. "Alex, no!"

Everyone watched as Alex's buddy Travis entered the phone store and was suddenly at Alex's side.

"Dude, Addie is here! You're gonna have to talk to her now," Travis said.

Alex turned nervously and saw Addie and her friend Tara looking at phone cases. He shook his head.

"This is so not happening. Every time I try, I screw it up—she's gotta think I'm crazy by now."

Gene realized it was now or never. "We have to help him connect to Addie!" Gene cried. "If we can do that, Alex will know he needs us."

"But who can pull that off?" Hi-5 asked.

"The only Emoji who can express himself like no other Emoji," Jailbreak said, looking sweetly at Gene.

All the Emojis stared at Gene.

"What?" Gene asked. "You think the one who caused all this—me!—is gonna *save* us now?"

FLASH! A green light surged through the theater! Where the countdown clock had been, there was now an alert: Full data erase . . . 0.5% complete, 8%, 10% . . . The number kept rising.

"It's starting!" Smiler cried as she frantically tried to wake up the Superbot.

Gene looked at Jailbreak. "I don't know if I can get Alex to express himself to Addie."

Jailbreak gave Gene a serious look. "Gene, why do you think I'm not in the Cloud right now? When you told me how you felt, and showed me *all* you were feeling . . . you made me realize I'd rather be here with *you* than there all alone."

"I did that?" Gene said in a shocked voice.

Jailbreak nodded. "Now *Alex* needs *you* to show him how it's done."

Gene gave Jailbreak a proud smile. "Can you find a way to bypass this wipe and send a text from Alex's phone?"

Jailbreak grinned. "Aw. It's like you don't even know me." She ran to the scanner.

"We've got to hurry!" Gene shouted.

Apps were disappearing quickly from Alex's phone as the wipe continued. Jailbreak began hacking.

"Got it! We're a go!" she shouted.

Gene set himself up in a cube. He looked over at Hi-5 nervously.

"The last time I was in this cube, I screwed everything up."

"That's because you were trying to be someone you're not," Hi-5 told him. "Just do *you*, my friend. Do *you*."

Alex's phone was still on the counter as the wipe continued. Only one app was left before the Text app would be gone forever! Alex waited. And Travis leaned in.

"Dude . . . ," Travis whispered.

"Okay, okay. I'm just going to do it," Alex said.

Alex turned around to speak to Addie—and nearly ran right into her, because she was suddenly standing right in front of him!

"Ahh!" Alex said, startled.

"I got your text," Addie told him.

"My . . . huh?"

"The Emoji you sent me," Addie said, holding up her phone.

Alex was mortified. "Oh no . . . it's my stupid phone," he began.

Addie smiled. "It's . . . kind of the coolest Emoji I've ever seen." Addie held the phone up and showed Alex the text. It was Gene. And he was making all kinds of expressions and showing all kinds of emotions.

"Gene! It's you!" Jailbreak cried.

"He's seeing me," Gene answered. "Not Meh. Me! Gene!"

Alex couldn't stop staring at the Emoji. "That's . . .

weird. It's like this Emoji knows what's happening with me right now. A lot of feelings, all in one."

Addie smiled at Alex. A warm, sincere smile.

Just at that moment, everything in the theater started shaking. The deletion process had begun.

"We're too late," Smiler cried.

"No!" Gene shouted. "Alex, come on! Ask her!" Gene yelled.

All the Emojis watched as Alex took a deep breath. Then it all came rushing out.

"Hey, Addie/beforeyousayanythingmore/ Iwantedtosay/doyouwanttogotothedance-withme? There. Done."

Addie looked surprised.

"Oh! I . . . really wasn't sure how you felt about me. . . ."

The shaking in the theater was getting worse. All the Emojis held tight to one another, waiting for the end.

"Come on, Alex, make the connection!" Jailbreak said.

Alex gulped.

"I . . . well, I feel nervous. And happy. And scared. And I like you . . . and I'm freaked and I guess I don't feel only one thing . . . and I think that's okay . . . and . . ."

Addie smiled and pointed to the Emoji on her phone.

"You're him!" she said.

Alex grinned, looking at Gene on Addie's phone.

"Yeah . . . he kinda nails it."

Fish-Cake-With-A-Swirl came running over. "Um, hello? Can someone explain to me why we're losing the Loser's Lounge . . . ? Whoa!"

The whole theater started to disappear!

Gene, Jailbreak, and Hi-5 held tight to one another as they watched Alex and Addie.

"Yes," Addie said.

"Yes?" Alex repeated.

"Yes, I'll go to the dance with you. I'm glad you were finally able to ask me—you know, face to face."

"Yes!" Gene shouted.

Addie raised her hand for a high-five, but Alex had his hand ready for a fist bump.

"No fist bumps," Addie told him. "I like the classic high-five way better."

Alex grinned as he high-fived Addie.

"Oh great. If the Favorites section wasn't getting erased right now, I'd totally be back in there," Hi-5 complained.

Alex picked up his phone and called out to the phone technician.

"Hey, excuse me?"

But the phone technician was busy talking to another customer.

All the Emojis held one another as the shaking grew stronger. They were just about to be wiped.

"Say your good-byes, Emojis!" Smiler cried.

But Alex calmly removed the wire hookups from his phone himself—stopping the wipe!

The shaking inside the theater came to a sudden stop. The green light went out—leaving the theater dark for a moment.

"What's happening?" Gene whispered.

Inside the phone store, the technician returned and saw what Alex had done.

"Changed your mind?" he said. "Good call. We ran a check before we started. There's no malfunction anywhere on your phone."

Alex looked at his phone screen. At Gene.

"Yeah. It's weird but . . . there's something about this Emoji." He looked up at the phone technician. "I'm gonna hold on to it."

The lights came back on and cheers erupted from all the Emojis—for Gene!

Suddenly the word REBOOTING appeared on Jailbreak's screen, and the theater and all Textopolis began to be restored.

Gene was confused. He turned to Hi-5. "No malfunction? But . . ."

Hi-5 smiled happily. "That means . . . you're not a malfunction, Gene."

Gene hesitated. "Then I'm . . . what am I?"

Jailbreak shrugged happily. "You're . . . you!"

"And Dad? That means . . ."

"I'm thrilled," Mel said in his Meh voice. "I may take a while to show it, but trust me, I'm thrilled."

"I always knew there was nothing wrong with either of you," Mary Meh said.

All the Emojis cheered for Gene again.

"Gene! You did it! You saved us!" they cheered.

Gene looked at Jailbreak shyly.

"I didn't do it alone."

"And you won't be alone again. I mean . . . not if you think you can hack me hanging around."

Gene grinned and stepped closer to Jailbreak.

"I'm pretty sure I'd just be lost in the wallpaper without you."

Hi-5 laughed. "Get a cube, you two!" he said.

Mary Meh started a cheer. "Gene! Gene! Gene!"

All the Emojis joined in. "Gene! Gene! Gene!"

Gene's expression started changing like crazy. Excited. Happy. Grateful. He couldn't choose just one. And he didn't want to!

Chapter 16

Back to Work

The next morning, Gene and Jailbreak were among the swarm of Emojis gathering for work.

Jailbreak looked at Gene.

"I'm kinda nervous," she told him.

Gene was surprised. "Are you kidding?" he said. "Don't worry. You're going to do great. You were made for this job."

Jailbreak gave Gene a sweet kiss. Their eyes turned into hearts.

"Go get 'em!" Gene said.

"Thanks," Jailbreak replied.

Jailbreak left and Gene met up with Hi-5.

"Hey! Big day, Gene! Slap me some skin!"

Gene slapped all Hi-5's fingers. Then they walked together. They passed the Peace Sign Emoji.

"Hi-5, hey," she said in a breathy voice. "I've missed you."

"I thought you were dating Fist Bump," Hi-5 said.

"He's not very open," Peace Sign admitted. "Plus, his face looks like a fist."

She winked at Hi-5. "Call me sometime."

Gene and Hi-5 kept walking.

A Ram Tech bouncer stopped them.

"Sorry, guys, you're not on the list," he said.

Hi-5 and Gene exchanged a shocked look.

Suddenly the bouncer laughed. "Just kidding! Come on in! Gene, everybody's waiting for you."

Gene and Hi-5 smiled at each other as they passed through the velvet rope to the Favorites section.

"Go get 'em, buddy," Hi-5 said. "You deserve it."

The next Emojis Gene saw were his parents waiting for him.

"Gene, this is an overwhelming moment for your mother and me," Mel Meh said.

"We're beaming with pride and love," his mother told him.

"Mom, Dad—I've never felt it more from you. Even though it also seems like you couldn't care less," Gene told them.

Gene turned around to see a brand-new cube, just for him.

Smiler made the announcement. "I hereby declare a new cube for our newest Emoji—Gene! For when one expression just won't cut it!"

"Thanks, Smiler," Gene said. "I gotta say, that smile looks pretty genuine on you."

Smiler gave Gene a forced "sour grapes" smile and walked away.

"Thanks, everybody," Gene said. "There's nothing better than feeling like you have a place in the world that you love."

"Welcome to the big time, Gene," Poop Emoji shouted.

Suddenly a female voice came over the sound system.

"Emojis, to your cubes!" the voice said. It was Jailbreak! She was the new Lead Technician!

"We're out of pocket! We are out of Alex's pocket, Emojis!" Jailbreak turned to the Ram Tech. "We up and running?" she asked.

"Roger that," the Ram Tech said.

"Good, 'cause we have incoming," Jailbreak continued. "And it looks like it's going to be Gene, in three, two . . ."

"I'm ready for my close-up, Alex!" Gene said.

As he spoke, the scanner rotated and pointed at Gene. His cube lit up. Gene looked happy and confident. He was Meh no more! He was whatever he wanted to be, and that was just perfect.

It was time for him to express himself.